GANDHI

THE PATH TO GREATNESS

Lushin Dubey did her MSc. in childhood education (with emphasis on special education) from the US and has taught children with special needs in the US and in Delhi.

She is the director of two theatre companies, Kidsworld and Theatreworld. She has conducted workshops and staged many productions, in India and overseas. She has been the recipient of several national and international awards for the theatre and screen.

AF530346

This book on Gandhi is dedicated to my beloved father Gobind Hemraj Keswani, who taught me the value of truth and integrity amongst so, so many other things.

I miss you, dad ...

Copyright © 2010 Lushin Dubey
Illustrations © 2010 Scholastic India Pvt. Ltd.
Photographs © Dinodia Photo Library

All rights reserved.

Published by Scholastic India Pvt. Ltd.
A subsidiary of Scholastic Inc., New York, 10012 (USA).
Publishers since 1920, with international operations in Canada, Australia, New Zealand, the United Kingdom, India, and Hong Kong.

No part of this publication may be reproduced in whole or in part, or stored in a retrieval system, or transmitted in any form or by any means, electronic, mechanical, photocopying, recording, or otherwise without the written permission of the publisher.

For information regarding permission, write to:
Scholastic India Pvt. Ltd.
Golf View Corporate Tower-A, 3rd Floor,
DLF Phase V, Gurgaon 122002 (India)

First edition: June 2010
Reprinted: July, September, December 2010, August 2012 January 2013;
March 2013; August 2015 Feb 2020 **April 2023**

ISBN-13: 978-81-8477-466-5

Printed at Ram Printograph Delhi

Gandhi

The Path to Greatness

A SHORT BIOGRAPHY

Lushin Dubey

Illustrations by Priya Kuriyan

SCHOLASTIC
New York Toronto London Auckland
Sydney New Delhi Hong Kong

Introduction

Dear Children,

If you had been born a century earlier, or say sixty-two years ago, you would have seen him.

He was of a frail thin body but a steel strong mind! One was struck by his strength and stature. All the great intellectuals and leaders of his time looked up to him for advice and support for their ideologies. He was a leader of leaders. That is why he is the father of the nation. Mohandas Karamchand Gandhi.

A man of minimal needs in personal life, but great desires for his people. A selfless man, a Mahatma.

I was lucky that I was born earlier in the twentieth century and as a schoolboy could see and hear him from very close. His voice was feeble, yet stern and assertive. His eyes poured love and affection. I felt like calling him Bapu. The whole nation remembers him by the same name. You could too.

Gulzar

FOREWORD

'Generations to come, it may well be, will scarce believe that such a man as this one ever in flesh and blood walked upon this Earth,' Albert Einstein said of Mahatma Gandhi. In a world increasingly wracked by violence it is indeed difficult to envisage someone like Gandhi. But that is probably the very reason why it is imperative that we revisit the Mahatma's life and message again and again. And indeed it is a testimony to the man's greatness that contemporary art—film and literature—keeps going back to him, reinventing his message for the times we live in. Over sixty years after his death, and close to a century after his experiments with truth and non-violence, Mahatma Gandhi continues to be relevant.

Gandhi was not just a freedom fighter. He was not simply another national leader. He shaped the destiny of not only one nation but the whole world in the twentieth century, in effect altering the world order as it existed. He not only led a nation to its freedom, he was also instrumental in the collapse of imperialism. His example and the methods he employed in the pursuit of his objectives hugely inspired other great leaders like Martin Luther King in America and Nelson Mandela in South Africa. His influence went far beyond political victory over an imperial foe, venturing into areas of social and spiritual upliftment of mankind.

This is why it gives me great pleasure to write this foreword to Lushin Dubey's *Gandhi: The Path to Greatness*. Volumes have been written about him. Given the sheer extent of information available on Gandhi, it must have been a formidable challenge to write about him in a manner that sustains interest. What is particularly heartening is that she never loses sight of her target readership: young children. Lushin's book has that one characteristic the Mahatma would have approved of: simplicity. In simple, uncluttered prose she succeeds in creating a vivid portrait of Gandhi, while providing information that readers will find valuable. I am sure that this succinct introduction to a great life will inspire its readers to explore the life and times of Gandhi in greater detail. In that sense it is an important addition to existing literature on Mahatma Gandhi.

Sharmila Tagore

1

Moniya

Mohandas Karamchand Gandhi was born on 2 October 1869 in a small seaside town named Porbunder near Bombay. In those days, India was made up of little kingdoms which had some degree of self governance but were supervised and controlled by the British monarch. The town of Porbunder was in the kingdom of Kathiawad, and Gandhi's father was employed as prime minister to its ruling prince.

In his childhood, Gandhi was known as 'Moniya'. As the youngest member of a large joint family, little Moniya held a special position which he seemed to have enjoyed. Often, when his father was not at home, he would remove the image of the ruling prince and put himself in its place. This same boy was to go on to unseat the mighty British Empire from its throne in Delhi.

While Moniya was playful and without fear, he also proved to be shy of organised group games. The only time he would spring to life was when a quarrel arose among his friends. Then he would unhesitatingly step forward as peace-maker and mediator. Even in later life in politics, he only 'played' when he could assume a unique

role of his own making.

In school, Moniya's main concern was being a model of good behaviour. Once, an educational inspector came on a visit to his classroom. He set the students five words to write as a spelling test. One of the words was 'kettle'. Moniya misspelt it. His teacher—in order to create a good impression on the inspector—tried to tell him the correct spelling. But Moniya refused to take the hint. He turned out to be the only boy who had got a spelling wrong in the test. But in his own eyes, Moniya had triumphed by sticking to the truth. For him, being 'good' did not mean doing what

was expected by others, but what he himself felt to be right. In this, he was much influenced by his mother who was devoutly religious. A central part of his faith was to tell the truth always, no matter what the cost. Another was to show love and non-violence to everyone.

2

Youth: Moniya turns Mohan

One must not think that truth always came easy to him. The life of Moniya, known as Mohan during adolescence was turbulent.

Once he broke off a bit of gold from his brother's armlet to clear a small debt. Later, this misdeed began to trouble him. He hesitated before confessing it. For one, his father had a violent temper and was strict about moral issues. This scared Mohan. More than that, Mohan knew how much trust and confidence his father had put in him. But there was no way out. As a grown man, this is how he described it in his autobiography:

'I decided at last to write out the confession, to submit to my father, and to ask his forgiveness. I wrote it on a slip of paper and handed it to him myself. In this note, not only did I confess my guilt, but I asked adequate punishment for it, and closed with a request to him not to punish himself for my offence. I also pledged myself never to steal in future. I was trembling as I handed the confession to my father. He was then suffering from a fistula and was confined to bed. His bed was a plain wooden plank. I handed him the note and sat opposite the plank.

He read it through and pearl drops trickled down his cheeks, wetting his paper. For a moment he closed his eyes in thought and then tore up the note. He had sat up to read it. He again lay down. I also cried. I could see my father's agony. If I were a painter, I could draw a picture of the whole scene today. It is still vivid in my mind …

This sort of sublime forgiveness was not natural to my father. I had thought that he would be angry, say hard things, and strike his forehead. But he was so wonderfully peaceful, and I believe this was due to my clean confession.'- *The Story of My Experiments with Truth.*

We can see that fifteen-year-old Mohan is aware not only of how much better he feels but also how his confession affected his father who was not forgiving by nature.

Around this time, Mohan had a friend whose ideas were different from Mohan's. Mohan's family was vegetarian, but the friend convinced him that it was good to eat meat. There was a poem by a Gujrati poet Narmad that was popular amongst schoolboys. It went:

Behold the mighty Englishman
He rules the Indian small,
Because being a meat-eater
He is five cubits tall.

Mohan started going out with his friend to eat meat. As with everything else Mohan tried, he showed great determination. He did not like the taste of meat, and as he writes, every time he dropped off to sleep, 'it would seem as though a live goat were bleating inside' him. Still he continued for almost a year.

It would have deeply upset his parents to hear of this experiment, so Mohan had to keep it a secret. On the other hand, he could not live with a lie either. Finally, he decided that 'though it is essential to eat meat, yet deceiving and lying to one's father and mother is worse than not eating meat.' Mohan became a vegetarian once more. Only this time it was by choice rather than by convention.

In 1882, when he was only thirteen years old, Mohan was married to a girl of the same age named Kasturba. It was an arranged marriage, according to time-honoured custom. The two of them had been betrothed by their parents when they were still children. One can imagine that Mohan enjoyed the elaborate ceremonies with himself at centre stage. But soon he was to realise what a great evil child-marriage was. Indeed, he never quite excused his father—or society—for having married him at such a young age. Later in life, he campaigned against child marriage. But, for all that, he was a devoted husband.

3

Gandhi in London

His father died when Mohan was fifteen. Four years later, Mohan, leaving his young wife and baby boy in the care of the joint family, set sail for London to study Law in 1888.

At first, he was terribly homesick. For many nights he would stay awake, thinking about his family. Everything was strange—the people, their ways, and even their homes. Finding vegetarian food in London was also a challenge. For the first few weeks, he almost starved. But soon he discovered a vegetarian restaurant at

which he was able to enjoy hearty meals. Gandhi was told by other Indians in London that it was important for him to talk, dress and behave like a true English gentleman. This would be even more useful than the formal study of law, when he returned back to India as a barrister in the courts of the British Raj.

Gandhi went about the business with gusto. Whenever he undertook anything, he always did it whole-heartedly. He bought an expensive suit made in Bond Street, which was the centre of fashion in London. He acquired the popular chimney-pot hat. In India, the mirror had been a luxury used on the days when the family barber gave him a shave. Now Gandhi began to spend long periods every day before a huge mirror, learning to arrange his tie and struggling with his unruly hair. Though he did not have too much money Gandhi started to take dancing lessons. But in spite of his efforts, he could not dance rhythmically as he could not follow the piano and had no ear for western music. Gandhi decided to learn to play the violin instead. Very soon he ran out of money and had to cable his elder brother—now the head of the joint family—for more. They were sent to him promptly.

Then, quite suddenly, it struck Gandhi how silly the whole effort was. The thought of his struggling brother, who always sent him money when he asked, pained him. Moreover, he realised, that he came from a country where most people did not know what it was to go to bed with a full stomach. The whole affair of

trying to be an English gentleman began to look silly to Gandhi.

With Gandhi, any change of mind had to be reflected immediately in his day-to day life. He moved to a tiny room in a cheap part of London. He began to cook at home and to walk to work rather then use the tram or bus. Most of his time was spent on studies. Now that he had arrived at what was right, nothing could shake him. His worldly-wise friends still advised him to pick up London manners. But their advice fell on deaf ears. Gandhi would unflinchingly follow his own beliefs even when they went against what

society considered wise. That was the only way he knew how to live. His new life did not in the least appear dreary to him. He wrote that it 'was certainly more truthful, and his soul knew no bounds of joy.'

4

Gandhi in South Africa

M.K.GANDHI.
ATTORNEY.

Gandhi returned as a qualified barrister to India, but did not stay there long. His services were soon engaged by an Indian firm based in South Africa. He set sail from Bombay in April 1893.

His stay in South Africa began with an incident that showed him how life there was filled with racial discrimination. He was travelling in a first-class train compartment when a passenger came in and looked Gandhi up and down. The sight of a 'coloured' man in first class disturbed this passenger so out he went. Soon he was back with some railway officials. They told Gandhi, 'Come along. You must go to the third-class van compartment.'

'But I have a first-class ticket,' protested Gandhi.

'That doesn't matter,' said the official. 'I tell you, you must go. Or else I shall have to call a police constable to push you out.'

'Yes, you may,' Gandhi replied. 'I refuse to get out voluntarily.'

The constable came. Gandhi was bundled out on to the platform. His luggage was thrown out after him, and the train steamed away.

Gandhi sat out the bitterly cold night on the

platform, brooding over the incident. It would have been only too easy to take the next ship back to India. But should he not stay on and fight for his rights?

Gandhi felt no personal hatred for the constable, or the railway officials, or the passenger who wouldn't share the compartment with him. Their behaviour was only a symptom of the deep disease of colour prejudice. Gandhi resolved to try to root out the disease, even if he had to suffer hardships in the process.

At that time the South African government had taken several discriminatory measures against Indians living in the country. The

most important among these was a bill for compulsory registration. It forced all Indians to be fingerprinted. It gave the police the right to challenge people and even enter their houses for searches.

Gandhi gathered the Indians around him in a solemn pledge to resist the Bill. He called for a public meeting to burn the registration cards. The police beat up many people, including Gandhi. But inspired by Gandhi's words and beliefs, his supporters bore the police assault without lifting a finger. Indeed, the procession to the British jails looked like a joyous celebration.

Gandhi nicknamed the jails 'His Majesty's hotels' and invited everyone to go to them as cheerful guests. The response was tremendous. It left the British authorities nonplussed. They were used to dealing with violent mobs. But what was to be done when unarmed men and women came in huge numbers to court arrest? This was a new phenomenon.

Gandhi called it 'Satyagraha' ('Satya' means truth, and 'agraha' is force.) Its principal rule was that the enemy was not to be combated, but won over by non-violent resistance.

When the Boer War broke out in 1899 between the British Empire and the two independent Boer republics, Gandhi called off his movement, and formed an ambulance corps to nurse the wounded soldiers of the British army. This was on the grounds that a true Satyagrahi never takes advantage of an opponent when he is in a weak position.

For Gandhi, the struggle was much more than a means to secure rights for the Indian community. He wanted to transform both sides in the struggle. There was a need to imbue the Indians with a sense of self-respect. But Gandhi also desired to help the British find a cure for colour prejudice. The movement against racial discrimination lasted a long time and aroused worldwide public opinion. Ultimately the British were forced to withdraw the bill. To General Smuts, who was the principal representative of the British government, Gandhi sent a gift of a pair of sandals that he had made with his own hands in prison.

Years later, Smuts recalled, ‘It was my fate to be the antagonist of a man for whom even then I had the highest respect.’ As for the sandals, he said that he had ‘worn them for many a summer since then, even though I may feel that I am not worthy to stand in the shoes of so great a man.’

5

Gandhi in India

After twenty years in South Africa, Gandhi set sail for India in 1914. When he arrived in South Africa, he had been in his Bond Street suit and looking forward to a career as a barrister. The man returning to India was very different. His true vocation of a satyagrahi had become clear. He was dressed entirely in native garb. In South Africa, wrote Gandhi, 'he had found himself.'

Gandhi's activities in South Africa had already made him well-known. He was welcomed into the Indian Congress Party which had begun to demand Home Rule within the British Empire. The Congress consisted of largely-westernised Indian elite, and some of its early leaders were Bal Gangadhar Tilak, Bipin Chandra Pal, and Lala Lajpat Rai, among others. It however needed a wider base and a leader who could excite the whole country.

In one of his first public speeches in the Congress, Gandhi said:

'I compare with the richly bedecked noblemen [on the platform behind him] the millions of the poor. And I feel like saying to these noblemen: "There is no salvation for India until you strip yourselves of this jewellery and hold it in trust for your countrymen in India" ... Our salvation can only come through the farmers. Neither the lawyers, nor the doctors, nor the rich landlords are going to secure it.'

When he said this, Gandhi himself was wearing only a loin-cloth. He had spent a whole year travelling all over India by train—'third class'. The sight of the poverty in which many villagers lived cut into his very soul. He vowed to share their way of life. He gave away all clothing except for the loin-cloth worn by the poorest people. By this, he dramatically emphasised who he stood for. When asked why he travelled in the crowded, dirty third-class Gandhi simply replied, 'Because there is no fourth.'

It was not Gandhi's way to conduct reform from an armchair. Before long, he was in the indigo plantations of Bihar. He had gone there in response to an appeal from farmers, who lived in a slave-like condition under European planters and Indian landlords. Gandhi's plan was not to confront them but the owners of the plantations were alarmed.

They had him summoned before a judge who ordered him to leave the area. Gandhi refused. There was a hurried consultation among the jury, who proposed a compromise. They asked him to put up Rs 1,000 by way of bail and to be on parole for a month.

'I will not put up even one rupee for this purpose,' Gandhi replied.

The bewildered judge had no choice but to put him in jail, which was exactly what Gandhi had wanted. It brought home to the over-exploited peasants that if they braced themselves for sacrifices then they would become their own masters.

The effect was immediate. The poor peasants

crowded around his jail cell. This frail-looking man—who dressed and lived like them—had won their hearts. More importantly, he had transformed their hearts and imbued them with new courage.

Gandhi's arrest became national news. An embarrassed British government withdrew its sentence on him, and let him proceed with his inquiry. For several months, Gandhi stayed in the village with peasants. Many educated Indians came forward to help him. Gandhi insisted that they regard themselves as clerks, accurately reporting the statements of the peasants. Many had brought

servants and cooks with them. These were sent packing. To work with Gandhi, one had to live the simple, poor life of the people one claimed to represent. By the end, Gandhi had compiled such enormous and fair evidence that he was able to bring about the end of the unjust system in the indigo plantations.

His ceaseless activities soon put Gandhi into the forefront of Indian politics. The magic of his appeal confirmed his claim to leadership. Large masses of people turned out to listen to this man who spoke to them in simple, everyday terms about their problems.

On one occasion, peasants lay down on the railway tracks to stop his train for just a sight of him. They began to call him 'Mahatma' (meaning 'great soul').

Even among the educated elite, Gandhi proved irresistible. He was able to lead them away from their armchair discussions to join his down-to-earth movement. 'You people are always talking about revolution,' he told them. 'Why don't you join me? I am making one.'

One of his converts was the young Jawaharlal Nehru who was to later become India's first prime minister. Jawaharlal had studied at Cambridge and come back to India as a prosperous lawyer. When he fell under Gandhi's spell, he gave up his career as well as his fine clothes and expensive habits.

His distraught father, Motilal Nehru, went to Gandhi for a private confrontation. 'You have taken our only son,' he pleaded. 'Give him back to us and I will put my wealth at your disposal.'

Gandhi listened to him patiently but only shook his head. 'Not only do I want your son,' he said with a mischievous smile, 'I want you, and your wife and your daughters, and the rest of your family too.' And he got them, one by one, beginning with Motilal himself.

Gandhi's overriding concern was the salvation of the poverty-stricken Indian people. It was the poor who suffered most from the brutality of the colonial British rule, and it was on their account that he entered the struggle for Indian freedom. He followed the path of satyagraha, as he had done earlier in South Africa. There was to be no violence whatsoever.

Once, when he called for a strike, there was an astonishing response. All shops and offices across the country came to a standstill. But in one small town, some overzealous patriots beat up a British officer. Gandhi was so pained by this lapse in his movement that he undertook a twenty-one-day fast to atone for it. And his party members went out with garlands to greet British officers.

Gandhi was unshakably firm. He suggested that to return work and food into the hands of the Indian peasants, all foreign cloth be boycotted.

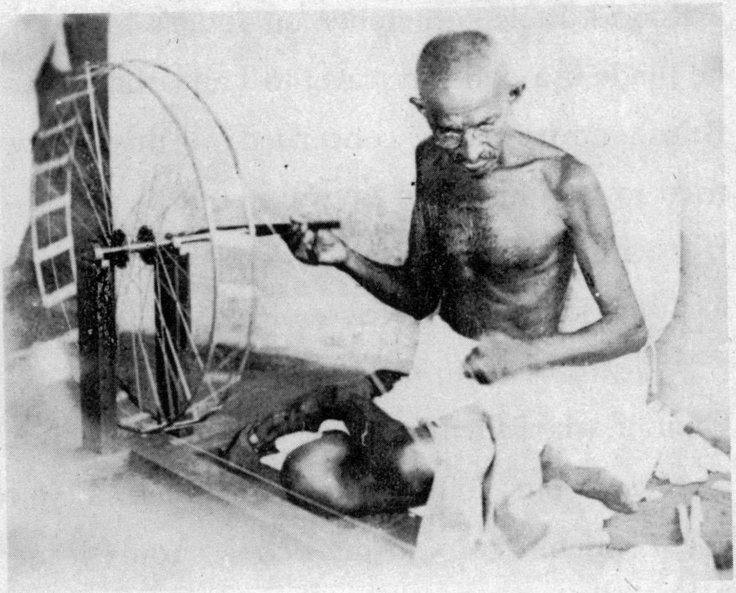

He went around the country presiding over big bonfires of foreign cloth. In their place, a spinning wheel was adopted and his large following began to wear only homespun cloth or khadi. Gandhi himself spent two hours every day on the spinning wheel. Simple as this might sound, it made several cloth mills in Lancashire close down.

When Gandhi went to England in 1930 for

a Round Table conference on India's freedom, he made it a point to travel to Lancashire. The British government, concerned for his safety, tried to stop him. But he wanted to be face-to-face with the angry crowd of workers who had lost their jobs solely because of him.

'Please listen to me for just a few minutes,' Gandhi asked them quietly. 'Give me a chance to present our point of view and then, if you like, condemn me and my people. You tell me that three million people are out of employment here, have been out of employment for several months. In my country, 300 million people are

unemployed at least six months in every year. You say that there are days when you can get only bread and butter for your dinner. But these people often go for days on end without any food at all.'

Though they had turned out to heckle him, the words of this little man went straight to their hearts. At the end, they hugged and cheered him.

It was on this occasion, too, that Gandhi was invited for tea to Buckingham Palace. After much inner debate, he decided to go in his loin-cloth and took care to get advance permission to

come without formal attire. Later a newspaper reporter asked him, 'Mr Gandhi, don't you think you were a trifle under-dressed for the occasion?' 'The British King,' Gandhi replied with a twinkle, 'was dressed well enough for both of us.' Little Moniya had now come of age as the Mahatma.

Gandhi's methods were often all the more startling for their simplicity. The idea of the salt satyagraha came about when the government imposed a law forbidding Indians to make their own salt. To Gandhi, this was a perfect symbol of how Indians were being exploited by their rulers. Salt was a necessity of life. There was no justice in making people dependant on a British monopoly for it.

Gandhi proposed to march with seventy-nine of his most trusted followers to the coast where salt lay free for the taking on the sand. It was an epic march of … 240 miles.

Gandhi was sixty-one but he had never been

in better shape. For over twenty-four days he walked, stopping at every village on the way to remind people of their duty of non-violent non-cooperation.

By the time he reached the coastal town of Dandi, his small, strange army had swelled to several thousand. Then, after a night of prayer, Gandhi stooped down and picked up a pinch of salt from the sand. As if waiting for this signal, huge crowds of men, women and children swept down to the sea to gather salt all along India's

coastline. It was a disobedience of British laws on a scale no one had ever imagined. The police assaulted Gandhi's followers who bore their injuries without so much as a complaint.

Ultimately Gandhi was to triumph. In 1947, the British left India. Without doubt, Gandhi had played the dominant role in winning India's freedom.

6

The Mahatma

The stakes for which Gandhi really played were much bigger. In between two World Wars he strove to show that there are higher things than military force. By the force of love and truth and non-violence, he over powered the greatest military power on earth. Even for India, Gandhi was not merely in pursuit of freedom. It was the quality of that freedom that concerned him most. He constantly 'turned the searchlight upon himself and his countrymen.'

Among the Hindu community there is a group

of people who were known as 'untouchables'. They are looked down on and not even allowed to draw water from the same well. These untouchable communities lived on the fringes of society and did menial work, such as scavenge.

Though he was a devout and high-caste Hindu, Gandhi described this practice as 'a blot of sin' upon the Hindu religion. His whole life was a ceaseless crusade against it. He founded several communal living centres in which the 'untouchables' were admitted as regular inmates who shared and lived equally with everyone. Gandhi used to call them 'Harijans' (children

of God). When on a trip to south India, he was taken to some ancient temples, he refused to enter them because their doors had been closed to 'untouchables' over the ages. 'There can be no God here,' Gandhi sharply told the priests around him.

Another matter of deep concern for Gandhi was the animosity between Hindus and Muslims. He believed in the universal brotherhood of man. At his daily prayer meetings, passages from the scriptures of every major religion in the world were recited. Gandhi tried to make their common message of love and peace stand out.

When the British talked of partitioning India along Hindu-Muslim lines, Gandhi was deeply upset. 'You will have to divide my body before you divide India,' he said.

In this, he was not to have his way. The eve of Independence was sorrowful for this man who had—almost single-handedly—made it possible.

For along with Independence, came partition. India into India and Pakistan. Savage Hindu-Muslim riots broke out as each group tried to flee from the region where it was a minority. In the northwest, about four million people were killed.

But in the border regions of the northeast, there was a strange calm. Gandhi had arrived. With two women satyagrahis, he set out on a walking tour. He held himself out as a simple sacrifice which would have to be made if any killings took place. From village to village Gandhi walked, calling upon the leaders of the Hindu and Muslim communities to embrace each other. And he succeeded!

When Gandhi returned to Delhi, the capital of the newly-born India, he was deeply distressed by the riots that had taken place there. He lived either in an untouchables' colony or a tiny, sparse guest room provided by a friend. Gandhi announced that he would go on a 'fast unto death' until the riots stopped. He came close to death's door but the riots ceased.

A few days later, while Gandhi was on his way to the daily prayer meeting, a Hindu fanatic, Nathuram Godse—who had been enraged with Gandhi's sympathy for the Muslims—shot him dead.

Gandhi was seventy-eight years old. His next plan was to march over a thousand miles to West Pakistan on a pilgrimage of love and peace. But this, alas, was not to be.